Wizzbang Wizard

Bubble Trouble

Scoular Anderson

HarperCollins *Children's Books*

for Fergus, Ruairidh, Katie and Charlotte

First published in Great Britain by HarperCollins *Children's Books* 2006
HarperCollins *Children's Books* is a division of HarperCollins*Publishers* Ltd
77-85 Fulham Palace Road, Hammersmith, London W6 8JB

The HarperCollins *Children's Books* website address is
www.harpercollinschildrensbooks.co.uk

1

ISBN-10 0-00-719006-9
ISBN-13 978-0-00-719006-5

The author and illustrator assert the moral right to be
identified as the author and illustrator of the work.

Printed and bound in England by Clays Ltd, St Ives plc

chapter one

Near the little village of Muddling, at the very end of Lumpy Lane, was a very strange house. Sometimes there were spots on the roof and sometimes there were stripes. Some days the walls were green and sometimes they changed to blue. For this was a wizard's house and it was a magical place to live.

A young wizard called Freddy Frogpurse stayed there, but the house really belonged to his Great Uncle Sneezer Frogpurse. He had gone off on a World Wide Wizard Walk so Freddy was looking after the place for him. Freddy was also supposed to be learning about magic so he could become a great wizard, too.

Freddy was in Great Uncle Sneezer's wizard room. There were shelves stretching right to the ceiling, stacked with books about magic. The cupboards were overflowing

with bottles of magic potions.

Freddy stood at a table with his sleeves rolled up and an apron on. The table was covered with bottles and Freddy's hands were covered in soap. He carefully tipped the contents of a blue bottle into a red bottle. He gave the red bottle a little shake. He added something from a green bottle. He gave it a stir with his magic wand. He held the bottle up and peered at the stuff inside.

"That looks about right," he muttered.

Just then, there was a scratching noise at the door.

"Master Freddy?" said a voice. It was Odds-and-Ends, Great Uncle Sneezer's house dragon who had been left to keep an eye on Freddy.

"Have you finished yet, Master Freddy?" Odds-and-Ends asked.

"Er... just a minute," said Freddy. He pulled his apron off and threw it over the bottles. He wiped his hands on his tunic, leaving big soapy smears. He quickly opened a big book and propped it up in front of him. It was called the *Wizards'*

Handbook (Volume One).

"Come in, Odds!" he said.

Odds-and-Ends pushed open the door and flew down to the table. He glanced round the room.

"Have you really been reading all afternoon?" he asked.

Freddy nodded.

"Oh, Master Freddy!" said Odds-and-Ends, tapping his foot on the table. "You've got the book upside down!"

Freddy's face went red.

"Well..." he moaned. "It's a very boring book, Odds."

Odds-and-Ends shook his head.

"How do you hope to become a great wizard if you don't work?"

"But I have been practising magic," said Freddy eagerly. "Look what I've done!"

He whipped the apron from his bottles. He picked up a bit of wire which was bent in a loop and dipped it into the liquid in the red bottle. He put the wire to his mouth and blew on it gently. A big bubble slipped from the wire and floated towards the ceiling.

"Bubbles!" said Odds-and-Ends. "What's so magic about that?"

Freddy blew another two. The first one

was bright green and the second was blue and pink stripes.

"These are extra big bubbles," said Freddy proudly.

Odds-and-Ends chased after the bubbles. "They're quite impressive. Your friends in the village will love you for this. But it's still not proper magic!"

"Don't be such a fuss pot, Odds!" said Freddy.

He blew another bubble. It was even bigger than the first ones. It floated low over the table and bumped into a jar. It rose upwards, taking the jar with it, trapped inside.

"Wow! Look at that!" Freddy squealed with excitement.

He blew yet another bubble. This time, it was enormous. It wobbled across the room like a hippopotamus trying to dance.

Odds-and-Ends flew in

reverse to get out of

the way but he

wasn't quick enough.

A moment later,

he was swallowed

up by the bubble.

He hammered on

the inside with his little

paws but it didn't burst.

"Help! Master Freddy! Get

me out of here!" he called.

But Freddy was having a fit of

the giggles.

"You should see yourself, Odds!"
he gasped.

Odds-and-Ends' hot breath was steaming up the inside of the bubble. The dragon cleared a little patch in the steam with his paw and peered out.

"Master Freddy, you've gone too far!" he squeaked. "You must start learning to be a proper wizard. Nobody will want a wizard who just mucks around... with bubbles!"

Just then, there was a loud knock at the front door. Freddy left Odds-and-Ends floating around the wizard room and went to see who was there.

A very important-looking gentleman
stood on the doorstep. The very important

gentleman looked Freddy up and down. He saw soap smears on his tunic. He saw coloured stains on his fingers and smudges on his face. The important gentleman looked at the sign beside the door which said: "Doctor Sneezer Frogpurse – Grand Wizard", then looked back at Freddy.

"Is Wizard Frogpurse at home?" he asked.

"Yes," said Freddy.

"I'd like to speak to him, then," said the gentleman.

"You are speaking to him," said Freddy.

The gentleman twitched his nose.

"I was expecting someone... er... older," said the gentleman.

"I may look young but I'm really seventy-five. It's great what you can do with magic!" said Freddy, trying not to laugh.

The gentleman twitched his nose again.

"Then you must come with me to

Gribble Castle. I am Lord Gribble's secretary and Lord Gribble urgently needs a wizard for a very special task."

A broad smile spread over Freddy's face.

"Just a moment," he said.

Freddy dashed back into the house. In the wizard room, he grabbed one or two things from a cupboard and stuffed them into his wizard's bag. He lifted his wand from the table and stuck it into his belt. He turned to Odds-and-Ends, who was still trapped in his bubble.

"What did you say a moment ago, Odds? You said nobody wanted a wizard who just mucks around. Well, you're wrong. Lord Gribble wants me, so there!"

"Oh no, Master Freddy, don't go there!" said Odds-and-Ends, banging his little claws against the inside of the bubble.

Freddy stuck his tongue out at the dragon and went.

chapter Two

The secretary took Freddy back to
Gribble Castle. They went in a little
carriage which lurched from side to side
as it went over the potholes in the road.
As they passed through the village,

people came to their doors to watch. Freddy felt very proud. It wasn't every day that a wizard was summoned by Lord Gribble.

When they arrived at the castle, they went through the big wooden gates and into the courtyard. They got out of the carriage and the secretary led Freddy up to the great hall.

Lord Gribble was sitting at the table with his eyes closed. He was trying to cheer himself up with some music. The secretary gave a little cough. Lord Gribble opened his eyes. He waved a hand and the musicians stopped playing.

"Well? Did you find the wizard?"

"Er... yes, my Lord," said the secretary.

"Where is he then?" asked Lord Gribble.

"Here, my Lord," said the secretary and he pointed downwards.

Lord Gribble stood up and peered over the edge of the table. Freddy gave a little bow.

"But he's younger than my son!" said the astonished Lord Gribble.

The secretary just shrugged.

"Well, let's see what you can do, Wizard," said Lord Gribble. He led them back out into the courtyard. They walked across to where a horse was tethered to a post.

"Next week my son has... er... an important task to perform," explained Lord Gribble. "He needs a really special horse. This is Emperor, the biggest, strongest horse I have, but sometimes he's a bit slow and sluggish. I want him to be nimble and fast as well as strong. I'm sure you must have some little magic thing you can do to make this happen, Wizard."

Freddy looked up at the horse... and the horse looked at him. Freddy didn't like

horses much. He realized now that he had made a big mistake. He should never have come to Gribble Castle. Odd-and-Ends had been right as usual.

Freddy didn't know any spells that would make a huge horse nimble and fast.

"What are we waiting for, wizard?" asked Lord Gribble.

Freddy decided to look as if he knew what he was doing and maybe an idea would come to him. He pulled his wand from his belt and gave it a polish on his sleeve. He blew on the end of it with his breath and gave it another polish. He twiddled it in the air then stuck it back in his belt.

Freddy opened his bag and rummaged around among the things he had thrown in there in his hurry to leave the house.

He lifted out a leather bottle and pulled out the cork, sniffing the contents. They smelled disgusting. Just then, he realized that Emperor was having a sniff, too. Freddy looked up and saw a set of yellow, horsey teeth. The teeth closed round the bottle and snatched it from Freddy's hands. Emperor chewed the leather bottle for a few seconds then swallowed. He burped loudly.

"Oh no!" said Freddy to himself in panic.

"What was in that bottle? Think! Think!"

He made a list of what it might be.

1 *Shrinking potion for Widow Wainscott's pig Clementine.*

(So that Clementine would fit into her new, smaller pen.)

2 *Potion for changing beans into cucumbers.* (Because Tom Feather had bought the wrong seeds for his vegetable plot.)

3 *Sleeping potion for the owl in Mistress Marble's tree.*

(To stop it keeping her awake at night with its hooting.)

But the horse didn't shrink or turn green or fall asleep. It opened its mouth and went **"Woof**

Woof

Woof"

Freddy suddenly remembered what was in the bottle.

4 Potion for making any animal act like a dog.

(Because little Lucy Limpet was given a rabbit for her birthday and she really wanted a puppy.)

"Woof!" went the horse again.

Freddy glanced up at Lord Gribble. His mouth had dropped open and he was staring at the horse with a puzzled look on his face. The horse gave a little skip then went galloping off round the courtyard, sniffing the ground. It chased some sparrows then came skipping back. It stopped in front of Lord Gribble, wagging its tail and panting.

"Gerwoof!" it said.

A broad smile slowly spread across Lord Gribble's face.

"I like this, Wizard!" he said. "Emperor is making strange noises but I've never

seen him so nimble on his hooves. You have done well! But don't go yet as I have another task for you to do."

Chapter Three

Lord Gribble snapped his fingers and two guards came running into the courtyard. One was tall, one was small. The tall one was carrying a big shield with an eagle painted on it. The small one was holding a long lance.

"You know what happens at a tournament, don't you, Wizard?" asked Lord Gribble. "Two knights put on armour then charge at one another with lances. They aim to hit one another's shield. Well, I want you to put a spell on the lance so that whoever is holding it hits the shield with the eagle on it every time."

Freddy had no idea how to do what Lord Gribble asked. He hadn't even reached the end of the first chapter of volume one of the *Wizards' Handbook* (fifty volumes) which he was supposed to read while his Great Uncle Sneezer was away. Then he remembered a little spell he used last winter when he was aiming snowballs at his pals. Now it was a lance not a snowball, but that might not matter.

Freddy closed his eyes, waved his wand and muttered the spell.

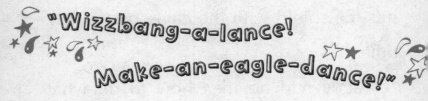

"Wizzbang-a-lance! Make-an-eagle-dance!"

The lance gave a little quiver then suddenly shot across the courtyard at great speed. The small guard hung on for dear life.

"WaaaAAAAaaagh!" he yelled, as he sped past Lord Gribble. The lance was just about to hit the eagle when the tall guard took fright and dived out of the way.

Then the lance swooped up towards a
crow that was sitting on the castle wall.
The crow flew off and the lance broke in
half against the wall with a loud crack.

The small guard fell to the ground with a thump.

"That was very impressive, Wizard," said Lord Gribble. "Though the aim needs to improve." He turned and whispered to his secretary. "I'm fed up listening to Baron Bricknoze boasting about how wonderful his son Bart is. Now, with the help of the wizard, we have a strong yet nimble horse and a lance that is sure to hit its target on the day.

Now my son Gordon is bound to win the tournament against Bart Bricknoze."

"But what if the magic fails, my Lord?" asked the secretary nervously.

"Then we'll know who to blame!" said Lord Gribble. "See the wizard out!"

A moment later, the big gates of Gribble Castle banged shut behind Freddy. He looked up and there was Odds-and-Ends, hovering in front of him.

"How did you get out, Odds?" Freddy asked.

"The bubble burst – eventually," said the dragon. "But what have you been up to?" Freddy told him what had happened.

"Master Freddy, the eagle on the shield is the coat of arms of Baron Bricknoze! Everyone knows the Baron is a terrible bully. If he finds out you've helped Lord Gribble's son win the tournament, you'll be in terrible trouble."

"Well... I didn't have much choice... I..." Freddy didn't say any more because

Odds-and-Ends suddenly flew in front of him, blowing sparks through his nostrils.

"Look out, Master Freddy!" squeaked the dragon.

It was too late. A big, fat book fell from the tree above them and hit Freddy on the ear.

"Ouch!" cried Freddy as the owner of the book fell, too, and they all landed in a heap on the ground.

"Sorry, Wizard. Sorry, Dragon," said the owner of the book.

"Who are you?" asked Freddy, rubbing his head.

"I'm Gordon, Lord Gribble's son. I slipped off a branch."

"What were you doing?" asked Freddy.

"I was sitting up a tree reading my

book and hiding from my dad," said Gordon, heaving a big sigh. "He wants me to fight Bart Bricknoze in a tournament but I'm no good with horses or lances."

"Well... I need to have a word with you about that," Freddy said nervously. "There's no need to hide now. I think you might have a very good chance of winning because—"

Gordon held up his hand. "Thanks for your support. But I don't stand a chance and Baron Bricknoze says that my dad must spend a month in his dungeon if I lose. You're right. I shouldn't be hiding in a tree like a coward. I'll go and do my best to please my dad. I hope you'll come and cheer me on."

Then Gordon picked up his cloak and started back for the castle.

Odds-and-Ends blew a few more sparks from his nose.

"Master Freddy, now you're in a right pickle! If your magic doesn't work and Gordon loses, Lord Gribble will be locked up. If Bart loses, he will probably find himself in his dad's dungeon. If Baron Bricknoze finds out you have helped Gordon..."

"I will end up in Baron Bricknoze's dungeon." said Freddy.

"You've got it!" said the dragon sharply.

chapter four

The day of the tournament arrived.

Freddy came out of the wizard room where he had been hiding all week.

"I have come up with a clever plan, Odds," he said. "I'll put the same spell on

Bart's lance, too. They will hit one another's shield and they'll both win!"

Odds-and-Ends wiggled his ears unhappily.

"I think that could just make things more difficult," said Odds-and-Ends.

"You are such a fusspot, Odds!" said Freddy. "Come on! We're going to be late!"

The tournament was held in the broad field outside Baron Bricknoze's castle. There was a big tent at each end of the field. Above one tent there was a flag with a picture of an eagle on it – the Bricknoze coat of arms. Above the other tent was a flag with a lion on it – the Gribble coat of arms. Crowds of people

had come from the villages all around to watch the tournament. A wooden grandstand had been built for important people.

There was a fanfare of trumpets as Baron Bricknoze and his wife took their seats at one end of the stand. Lord and Lady Gribble sat down at the other.

"Well, Gribble!" shouted the Baron. "Are you looking forward to your stay in my dungeon?"

Lord Gribble gave a sly smile.

"Let's lay a bet, Bricknoze!" he said. "If my son loses, not only will I go into your dungeon, you can have my castle

as well. But if your son loses, your castle
is mine."

"Agreed!" Baron Bricknoze said, with
a loud laugh.

There was another fanfare
of trumpets. Bart Bricknoze,
the Baron's son, swaggered
out of his tent wearing a
shiny suit of armour. He
leapt on to his horse
and gave everyone a
broad smile.

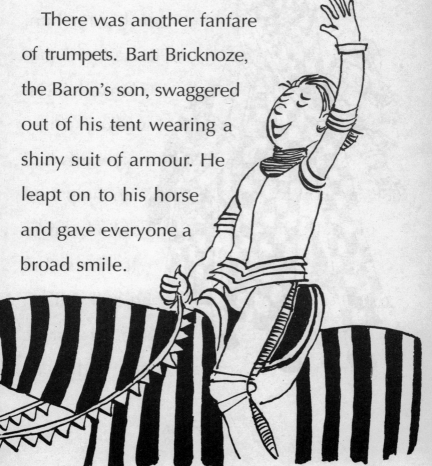

A servant handed him up his helmet then his shield and lance.

Gordon's suit of armour was too big for him. It clattered and clanked as he walked. Three servants had to help him climb on to the horse but he still fell off twice. At last he was on and as he clung to the back of the frisky Emperor, he found it hard to hold his lance and shield.

The referee stepped forward, raised his hand then dropped it again. The two young knights began to gallop towards one another.

A great cheer rose up from the crowd as the two knights drew closer and closer.

The spell on Gordon's lance should make it aim for the eagle on Bart's shield, Freddy thought to himself. Now he had to put a similar spell on Bart's lance. Freddy quickly pushed his way to the front of the crowd. He snatched his wand from his belt and pointed it at Bart's lance.

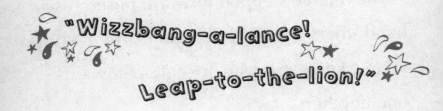

"Wizzbang-a-lance! Leap-to-the-lion!"

Things didn't go to plan.

Bart and Gordon were just about to meet when Gordon began to fall off his horse again. He dropped his lance and shield as he made a grab for his horse's neck. At that moment, Bart Bricknoze took to the air. He flew over his horse's head and headed for Gordon's tent. Only

Freddy knew why. Bart's lance was heading for the lion on the flag above Gordon's tent.

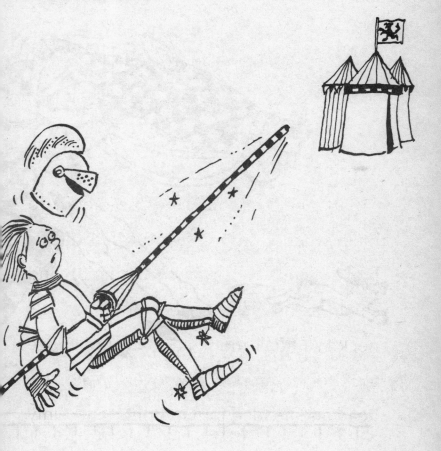

At the same time, Gordon's horse spotted
a rabbit at the far end of the field.

"Woof! Woof!" he snorted. Emperor was a horse who thought he was a dog and set off to chase the rabbit.

At first, Baron Bricknoze's face turned red. Then it turned purple. Lord Gribble's face turned pure white. They both looked one way to see Gordon vanish into the distance.

They both looked the other
way to see Bart still clinging to
the flagpole of Gordon Gribble's tent.
Then the Baron began to roar with
laughter.

"Well, Lord Gribble, there's no doubt who the winner is. My son has scored a bull's-eye by sticking his lance through the coat of arms on your flag. Your son has galloped off! You will have to spend a little time in my dungeon!"

Chapter Five

The next day there was a loud knock at the door of Wizard's House.

"It must be Baron Bricknoze!" said Freddy and he dived behind the sofa.

"Don't worry," said Odds-and-Ends, as

he peered out of the window. "It's only Gordon Gribble."

Freddy went to the door and let him in.

"I'm so sorry, Gordon," said Freddy. "It was my fault that the tournament was a disaster yesterday."

"It wasn't really your fault," said Gordon. "I know my dad put you up to it. The guards told me. Now I've come to ask if you will use your magic to get Dad out of the dungeon in Bricknoze Castle."

"I can't do that, I'm afraid," said Freddy. "That's really Big Magic. I'm no good at it."

"Then Dad will have to stay there for a month – maybe even more," said Gordon with a big sigh. "The Baron's men have already taken over our castle and my mum has gone off to stay with her sister Mildred."

"Wait! I think I ought to help you out

of this mess," said Freddy. "A clever plan has just come into my head!"

Odds-and-Ends wiggled his ears in dismay. "I hope it's better than the last one."

"This is what we'll do," said Freddy. "Firstly, we'll deal with the guards. Odds, you will fly into Baron Bricknoze's castle with the sleeping potion I made for the owl in Mistress Marble's tree. Scatter it on the floor of the guard room. That will put the guards at the gate out of action. Then Gordon and I will climb over the castle wall..."

"How on earth do we do that?" asked Gordon.

"Don't worry, I know a spell for making a rope do tricks. Once we're inside, we'll get your dad out of the dungeon somehow."

"Oh, Master Freddy!" said Odds-and-Ends, blowing out a hot puff of smoke. "It's very dangerous, but I'll help."

They waited until it was nearly dark
before they set out for the castle. They
crossed the drawbridge over the moat
and, when they reached the gates, Odds-

and-Ends flew up and over the castle
wall. The guards were in the guard room,
sitting round a table having their supper.
They were making so much noise they

didn't notice the little dragon flying low under the table. Odds-and-Ends scattered the sleeping potion between their feet.

A minute later, the guards began to yawn. A minute after that, their eyelids began to droop. In another minute, all the guards fell face down into their plates and were soon snoring their heads off.

"It's done, Master Freddy!" said Odds-and-Ends, as he appeared over the castle wall again.

"Right!" said Freddy. "Into the castle we go!"

He laid the long rope he had brought with him on the ground. He pulled his wand from his belt and cast a spell.

"Wizzbang-a-rope-grow-tall! Climb-up-the-castle-wall!"

The rope gave a twitch then one end shot up to the top of the castle. Freddy grabbed the other end and began to climb.

"Quickly! Follow me before the spell fades!" he called to Gordon.

The rope swayed and swooped as the two climbed.

Odds-and-Ends sat on a nearby windowsill and watched anxiously. Unfortunately, he was sitting outside the window of Baron Bricknoze's bedroom.

Now there were three things that terrified the Baron:

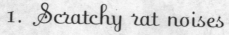

1. Scratchy rat noises
2. Fluttery bat wings
3. Creatures with pointy claws

Just as the Baron slipped into bed beside his wife, he heard a horrible scratching noise over by the window. By the light of the moon he saw a creature on the windowsill flapping its wings and waving its pointy claws.

The Baron let out a terrified gurgling noise. His wife screamed and the pair of them leapt out of bed and down the stairs.

chapter Six

By the time Freddy and Gordon got down to the inner courtyard, the whole castle was awake. There were shouts and yells and the sound of clattering feet on stairs. Guards were running from every corner with flaming torches and swords in their hands.

"The dungeon's over here, Master Freddy!" squeaked Odds-and-Ends.

They ran to a dark corner of the courtyard where they saw an iron trapdoor in the ground. Luckily, it wasn't locked so they heaved it open. They found a ladder nearby and threw it down into the darkness.

"Dad!" yelled Gordon. "Dad! Are you there?"

A moment later, Lord Gribble's face appeared out of the gloom.

"Gordon!" he cried. "How did you get here?"

"There's no time to explain," said Gordon. "Climb up the ladder! As fast as you can!"

"The guards are coming this way!" squeaked Odds-and-Ends.

"Quickly, up these stairs!" said Freddy.

They rushed up the stairs and along a corridor, but the guards were right behind them. Freddy stopped and turned round.

"Stay back!" he shouted, as loudly as he could.

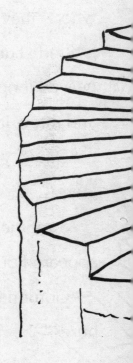

Freddy rummaged in his bag. He had an idea.

The guards stopped for a moment. Freddy brought out a bottle and a little bit of bent wire. He uncorked the bottle and dipped the wire into it. He put the wire to his mouth and began to blow.

"Bubbles!" said one of the guards. "The silly little wizard is blowing bubbles!"

The guards roared with laughter. One of them poked at a huge bubble with his spear as it floated towards him. It didn't burst. It just swallowed him up. A second later, three puzzled guards were floating around in bubbles. They blocked the corridor so the other guards couldn't move.

Freddy ran and caught up with the others. Now there was another problem. They had reached the top of the highest tower in the castle.

"It's a pity we left the rope behind," said Gordon.

"We're trapped!" wheezed Lord Gribble, as he tried to get his breath back.

"Perhaps not," said Freddy. He rummaged in his bag again. "It's another bubble to the rescue!"

He pulled out his

bottle of bubble mixture. He blew a really enormous bubble, which quickly swallowed up both Gordon and Lord Gribble. Then he waved his wand.

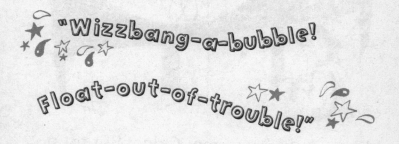

"Wizzbang-a-bubble! Float-out-of-trouble!"

The huge bubble toppled off the castle wall and floated off into the darkness. The last thing Freddy saw was the terrified look on Lord Gribble's face.

"I just hope it doesn't float towards any trees," said Freddy. "Now you'll have to

blow a bubble for me, Odds. But try not
to fill it with smoke."

The dragon blew a bubble the size of a
pea.

"You'll have to do better than that!"
said Freddy, as the guards appeared at
the top of the tower.

"There's no bubble mixture left, Master Freddy!"

"I'll have to hitch a lift with you, then, Odds," said Freddy, grabbing the dragon's feet.

"Oh, you're far too heavy, Master Freddy!" said the dragon, spluttering out some sparks.

"Well, what will you say to Great Uncle Sneezer if he comes back and finds me locked in Baron Bricknoze's dungeon?"

"Oh, very well," said Odds-and-Ends. "Hold tight!"

Freddy jumped off the top of the tower while Odds-and-Ends flapped his wings furiously, but it wasn't much good. They were going down rather than along. Freddy let go and fell with a splat into the muddy moat.

chapter seven

A week after the escape from Bricknoze Castle, Freddy was outside the wizard's house, pulling his gown from the washing line. It had taken five wizzbang washes to get rid of all the smelly moat mud. He slipped on the gown and set off up Lumpy Lane. He wanted to see how Gordon Gribble had got on since his flight in the bubble.

As he passed Bricknoze Castle, he saw a lot of people rushing about. He couldn't resist having a closer look so he crept up behind a bush and peered across at the castle. Carts were rumbling out of the gate and across the drawbridge. They were piled high with furniture.

Suddenly there was a whirring of wings and Odds-and-Ends appeared.

"Is it safe for you to be here?" asked the dragon.

"I just wanted to see what was happening," said Freddy.

"The gossip is that Baron Bricknoze is going to live somewhere else," said Odds-and-Ends. "He thinks his castle is haunted by a monster with leathery wings and huge scratchy claws!"

The dragon blew a puff of smoke through his nose, which was his way of laughing.

"Fancy the bully being scared off by a little dragon!" Freddy laughed.

Just then, someone else appeared. It was Gordon Gribble, clutching a book under his arm.

"I was just on my way to see you," said Freddy.

"And I was just on my way to see you,"
said Gordon. "You'll be pleased to know
that my dad has agreed I'm better at
reading books than being a knight."

"I wish someone else was as keen on reading books as you," said Odds-and-Ends, looking hard at Freddy.

Freddy went bright pink. "I'll have finished reading volume one of the *Wizards' Handbook* by the end of the month, Odds. That's a promise!"

Don't miss more magical adventures in...

Wizzbang Wizard

Super Splosh

Freddy picked up his wand and twirled it round and round.

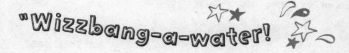

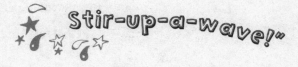

Freddy Frogpurse has come to his Great Uncle Sneezer's house to learn how to be a wizard. His dragon, Odds-and-Ends, nags at him to practise more, but Freddy just wants to have fun...

0-00-719006-9
www.harpercollins.co.uk

HarperCollins *Children's Books*